Getting Together

Carmel Reilly

Australia • Brazil • Japan • Korea • Mexico • Singapore • Spain • United Kingdom • United States

Getting Together

Fast Forward
Green Level 12

Text: Carmel Reilly
Editor: Johanna Rohan
Design: Stella Vassiliou
Series design: James Lowe
Production controller: Emma Hayes
Photo research: Michelle Cottrill
Audio recordings: Juliet Hill, Picture Start
Spoken by: Matthew King and Abbe Holmes

Acknowledgements
The author and publisher would like to acknowledge permission to reproduce material from the following sources: Photographs by AGE Fotostock/P Narayan, p9; Alamy/Bryan and Cherry Alexander, p13; Australian Picture Library/Corbis/Wolfgang Kaehler, p12; Getty Images/Hulton Archives, pp 14, 18; Image Bank, pp 21, 23/Richard Harrington, p19/Robert Harding World Imagery, p16/Stone, front cover, pp 1, 6, 10/Time Life Pictures, p3; Newspix/Jeff Herbert, p17; Photolibrary.com/Alamy/David R Frazier, p8/Chuck Mason, back cover, p22/Michael Sewell, p11/Steve Cicero, pp 4-5; Stock Photos/Masterfile/Kevin Dodge, p7/Peter Griffith, p20; Superstock/Purestock, p4; Territory Images, p15.

ISBN 978 0 17 012567 3
ISBN 978 0 17 012561 1 (set)

Cengage Learning Australia
Level 7, 80 Dorcas Street
South Melbourne, Victoria Australia 3205
Phone: 1300 790 853

Cengage Learning New Zealand
Unit 4B Rosedale Office Park
331 Rosedale Road, Albany, North Shore NZ 0632
Phone: 0508 635 766

For learning solutions, visit cengage.com.au

Printed in Australia by Ligare Pty Ltd
5 6 7 8 9 10 11 20 19 18 17 16

Evaluated in independent research by staff from the Department of Language, Literacy and Arts Education at the University of Melbourne.

Getting Together

Carmel Reilly

Contents

FAMILIES

People all around the world live in families.
A family is a group of people who live together.
Some families are big.
Some families are small.
Many people live in a family all the time.
Some people don't live with their family,
but they are still part of a family.

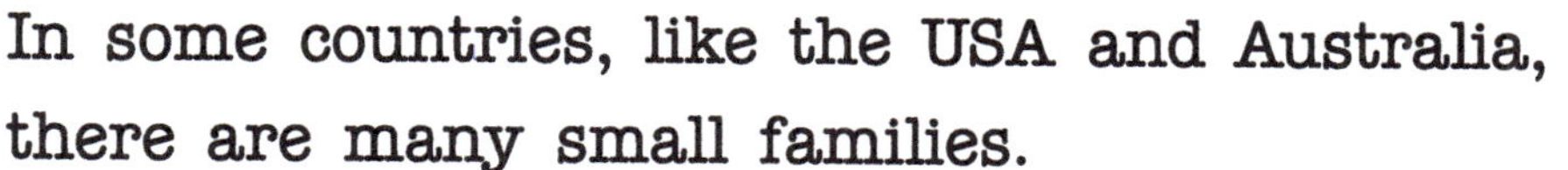

In some countries, like the USA and Australia, there are many small families.
A lot of families are made up of just the parents and one or two children, all living in the same house.
This kind of family is called a **nuclear family**.

a nuclear family

Chapter 2

EXTENDED FAMILIES

In other countries, families are very big.
Sometimes, grandparents,
or other people who are related,
live with a family.

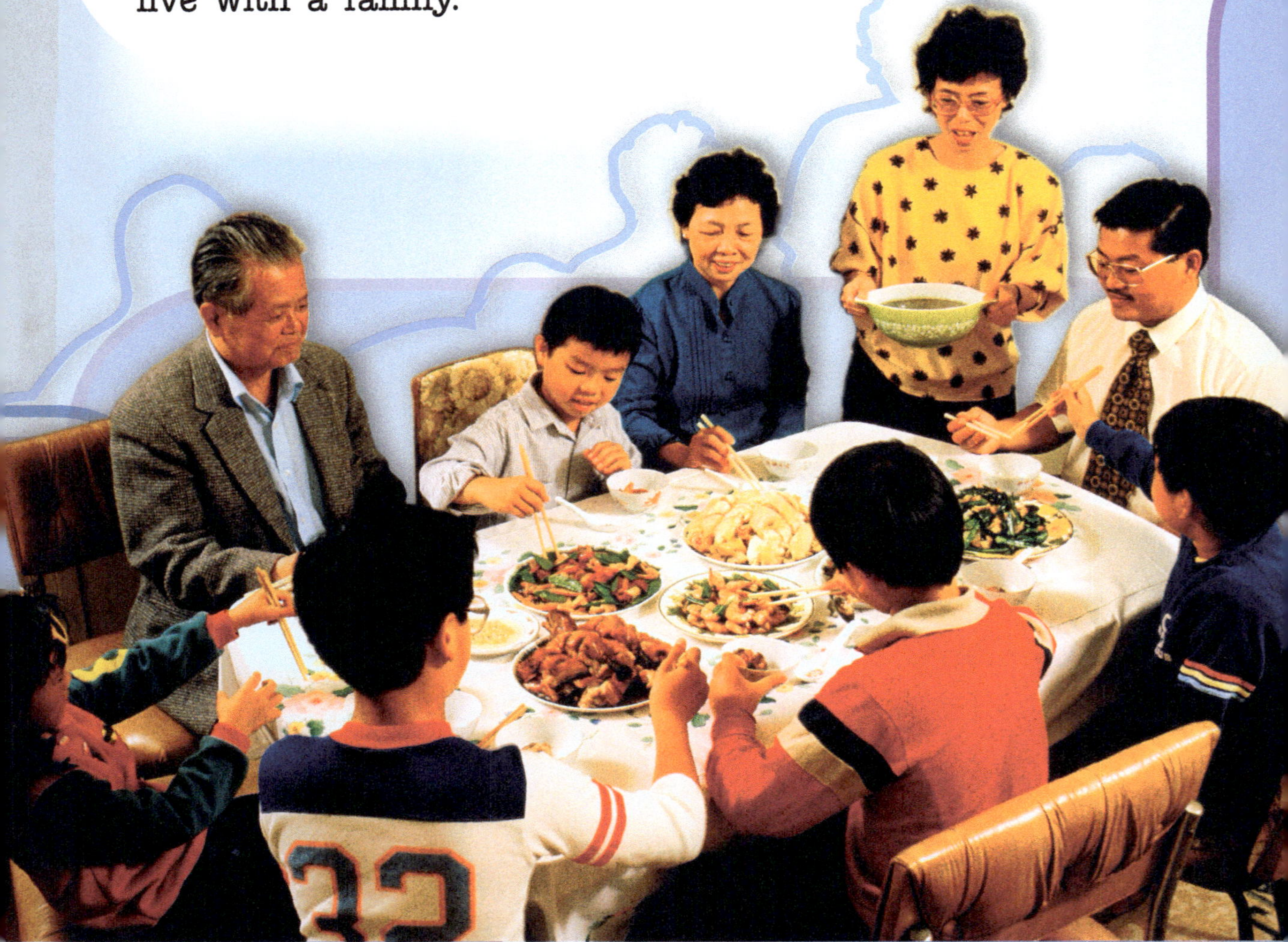

an extended family

Sometimes, two or more families
who are related
live together and make one very big family.
Families with more than just
a mum, a dad and children
are called **extended families**.

INDIAN FAMILIES

In India, many families are extended families. Most of the time, grandparents, parents and children live together in one house.

Running Words 164

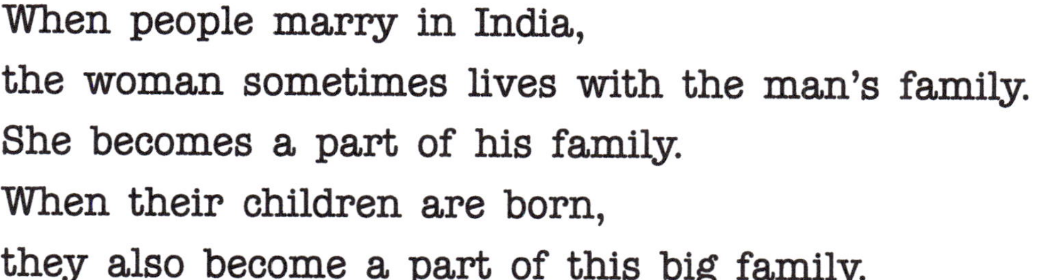

When people marry in India,
the woman sometimes lives with the man's family.
She becomes a part of his family.
When their children are born,
they also become a part of this big family.

son's wife
sister
son
son's child
grandmother
mother

INUIT FAMILIES

Inuit people live in small nuclear family groups most of the time.

Inuit are aboriginal people who live in Canada and Greenland.

Inuit people move around a lot to look for food. Being in a small group makes moving around easier.

Inuit people hunt together in small family groups, but their extended family is still very important to them.

Inuit people get together
in their extended family groups
to share food and to take care of each other.
They also teach their children about Inuit culture.

Chapter 5

AUSTRALIAN ABORIGINAL FAMILIES

In the past, most Australian Aboriginal people lived in extended families, too.

Sometimes, these family groups were made up
of only a few people.
At other times, they were made up
of hundreds of people.

Today, many Aboriginal people still live in big family groups.

In these groups, people share things and take care of each other. Everyone takes care of the children.

Chapter 6

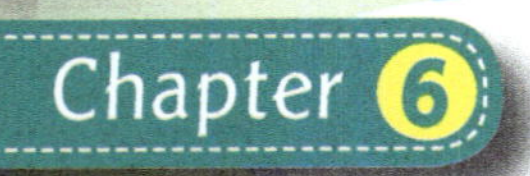

CHINESE FAMILIES

For hundreds of years, most families in China were extended families.
They were made up of grandparents as well as parents and children.

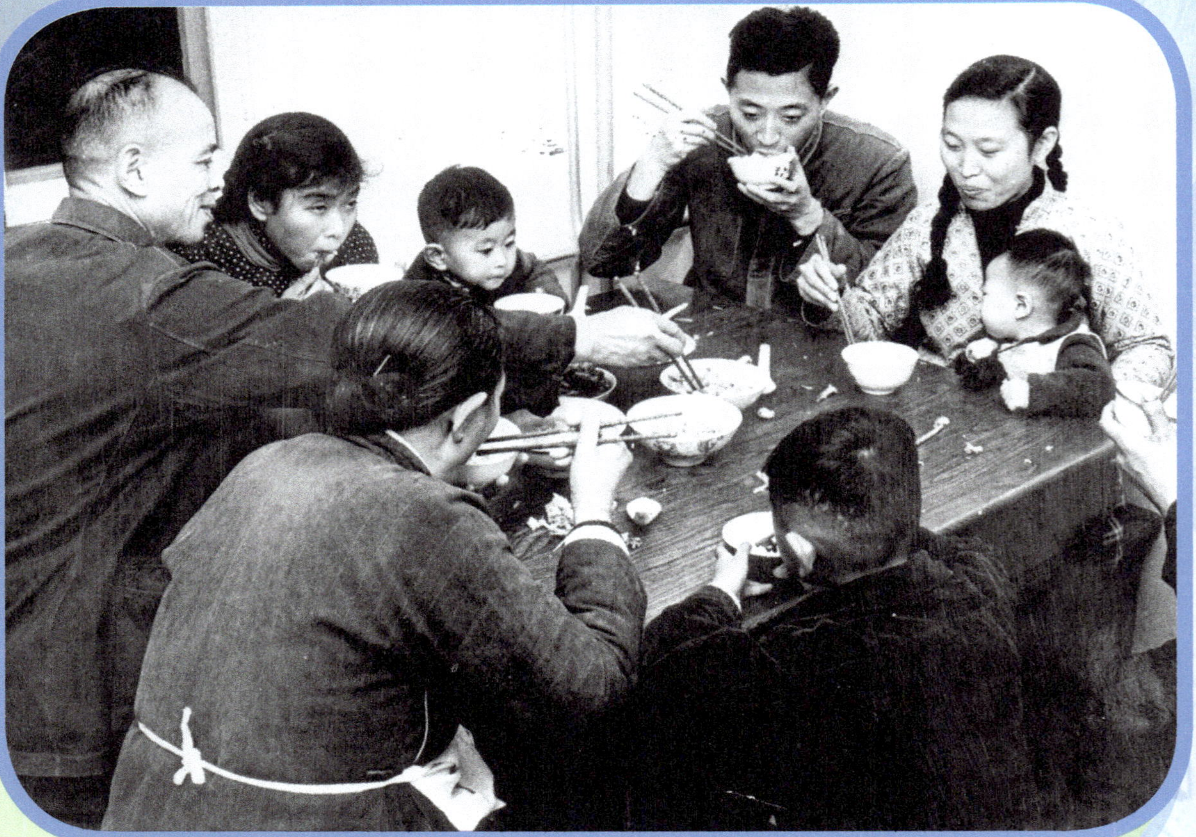

Sometimes, two or more related families lived together.
If they lived in the country, these families worked together on the land.

Today, families in China are much smaller. China is a very crowded country, and most families only have one child.

Also, most people's homes are small, and there isn't as much room for big families to live together.

Chapter 7

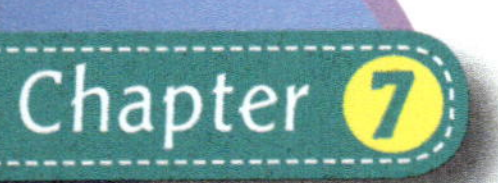

GETTING TOGETHER

Families around the world are different from each other.
But, big or small, some things are the same for all families.

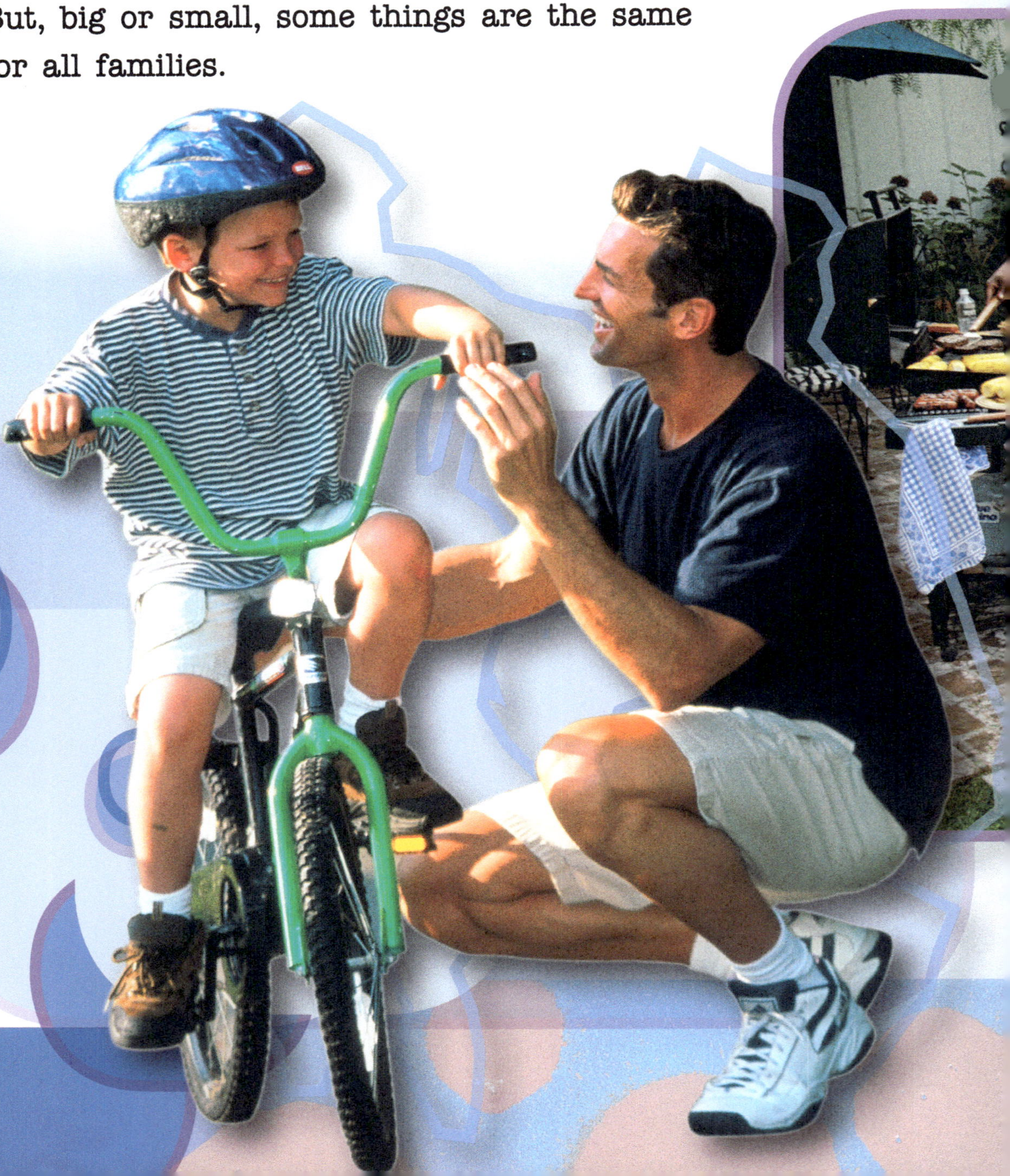

Families around the world get together to share things and to take care of each other.

Glossary

extended families large families made up of more than parents and children. Grandparents and other relatives make up an extended family.

nuclear families small families made up of just parents and one or two children

Index